Memoirs of a Pomsky

Beth A. Freely

Memoirs of a Pomsky
by
Beth A. Freely

Humans...

My master is a dumbass.

He has yet to figure out that in order to keep a woman you have to treat her right. Bringing a six pack of Pabst Blue Ribbon, Slim Jim's and pork rinds to her house to watch the stock car races and calling that a date is not going to get him a second one.

And honestly, how many times can you watch a car make a left turn? Even I get tired of making left turns chasing my tail! You gotta go a different direction just to make things interesting. Crash and burn into a wall. Something!

I feel like I need a doggy version of some addiction hotline for people with no dating skills.

I'm Delphine, by the way. I'm a teacup Pomsky with a full, soft coat, one blue eye and one brown, and an imposing bark.

"Yip. You do not bark. You yip. There is nothing imposing about your bark."

"I didn't ask for comments from the feline peanut gallery! Go away!"

Anyway...where was I? Oh yes. My master, he who has no play, is Grant Laslow. By day, he is the CEO of a midsized corporation specializing in pet stuff. I think. It's the only explanation for why there are always other animals in the building he works in. To be honest, the place smells like a barnyard and I bark my way through the cubicles, mentally urging Grant to get to his office. That's my safe haven. It doesn't smell like those other animals. It just smells like Grant and me.

But I digress. By night, Grant is the leader of The Drunken Outlaws Motorcycle

Club. This bunch of...enthusiasts like to ride around on their big bikes causing trouble for an unsuspecting bystander. They cause a ruckus everywhere they go, and their vehicles are loud.

Well, they used to be drunk. And they used to cause a ruckus. Their motorcycles are still loud. Don't get me wrong. These guys are big and menacing. Even Grant. And I'm pretty sure Perry and Doggo's masters have warrants. And most of them are covered in tattoos.

At some point in their motorcycle club heyday, they all stopped drinking and decided to raid a dog pound instead. I got adopted by mister big, tough, and sucks at love.

Oh, don't get me wrong. I'm his princess. I'm a highly pampered pooch that gets to sleep at the head of his bed on a satin pillow. I get the choicest pedigree food money can buy, all the best toys and I get to ride on his Harley cruiser in my little doggie pack with my own goggles and helmet. My life is wonderful.

"Your goggles look stupid. I'm just saying."

"No, they don't. They are fashionable. Go away, cat. This is my story."

"Да, да, верь во что тебе угодно."

"I will! I will believe what I want. Now shoo or I'll make daddy spray you with the water bottle!"

Please, ignore the cat. I'll tell you about him later.

As I was saying, my life is wonderful. Except when Grant starts lamenting over the fact that he's lonely. And he really wishes a woman would "get him."

I'm not sure what, exactly, she is supposed to be getting him, but whatever. When he gets in one of these moods, I get cuddled to the point of my near death. He gets his salty tears in my fur. I groom myself after he falls asleep and there is enough salt on my undercoat that I could rim a margarita glass.

But there is one woman who Grant likes. And he doesn't even know he likes her. I know he does. Even the cat knows he does.

"I have a name."

Memoirs of a Pomsky

"I'm ignoring you!"

I...to be fair, we...can hear his heart beat speed up and my doggie nose can smell the pheromones. And to be honest, I like her too.

Oh now, don't look at me like that. There have been a few prospective women I wouldn't have minded sharing my satin pillow with if she made my master happy. Okay, so maybe I didn't like Linda with the bleach blonde hair that smelled of patchouli and Ben-Gay. And I might have peed in Karen's boots when she made me sleep outside the bedroom because "dogs belong outside." But can you blame me?

Anyway...

Her name is Dallas, like the city in Texas. And she's a tattoo artist. Grant's gone to see her twice now and both times I could tell he was digging her. I adore her. She has gentle hands and knows where to scratch behind my ears to make me wiggle. She lets me sit in Grant's lap while she works on his arm and feeds me treats when he's not looking.

I only have one problem with Dallas.

His name is Ivan.

"That would be me."

Memoirs of a Pomsky

Ivan, The Russian Blue

The very first time Grant carried me into Pigments of Your Imagination, I wasn't sure if we were entering a tattoo parlor or a new age hippie den. You could smell the Nag Champa incense before you opened the door and the music playing over the loudspeakers inside was not what I expected. Grant listens to heavy metal...Dallas, some new age soothing music you could do yoga to. There were two chairs, one on each side of the room, and posters along the walls of animals and flowers that I am pretty sure glowed fun colors under a black light.

Dallas herself greeted us with a big smile and soft voice. Grant was carrying me in his arms, and I looked up to see this stupid grin on his face. He told her what he wanted, handed me to her and pulled off his leather jacket, showing her the spot on his muscular bicep where he wanted her to start the sleeve. She buried her face in my fur, told me I smelled good and carried me to one of the chairs. She set me down on a pet bed in the corner. It was soft and I figured I could catch a few winks.

Until I caught his scent. The undeniable odor.

Cat.

I looked around and saw him all loafed in the other corner. Only his eyes could be seen, gold and menacing. *"You stay over there, pal,"* I barked. I laid down on the pet bed.

"What are you?" the cat hissed.

"Superior to you," I answered. The bed stunk of cat, but I wasn't about to give up this cushy piece of heaven.

"Oh look, Ivan and Delphine are getting to know each other," Dallas said happily.

"Ivan? He won't hurt her, will he?"

Hurt me? Please. I will eat that feline for break...

"Ivan? No. He's a big softie. He's my big boy, cuddle bumps." Dallas reached down and scratched the top of his head.

Maybe not. Ivan stood and slowly walked over to me. Big boy, cuddle bumps was twice my size and could eat ME for breakfast.

"He's a big boy," Grant laughed as he watched Ivan languidly stretch, all claws out in a show. "He won't hurt my princess, will he?" He sat down in the chair, swinging his jean clad, booted legs up onto it and stretching out, getting comfortable.

"No. Well, maybe if he sits on her," she laughed.

Before I knew what was happening, Dallas was scooping me up off the bed and settling me in Grant's lap. *"Ha!"* I said to Ivan.

"Pft. Peasant." He settled on the bed and began licking his paws, making sure to show me all of his sharp claws before loafing up in the middle of the bed.

"Now, Ivan, be nice. She's a guest here," Dallas admonished gently. She reached down to scratch his ears before opening a drawer and getting a treat. She held it out to me as a peace offering. "So, I looked at the design you wanted. I can do it all in about seven sittings."

"I can do seven sittings."

I settled in Grant's lap, looking up at this new lady as she and my master talked. She had big blue eyes and a mess of sandy brown hair she kept pulled up in a messy bun. She had a nice figure, curvy and lush and I bet she was nice and soft to lay on. I looked at that thing on the floor and bet he knew if she was soft and comfy to lay on.

"So, I'll do this part tonight and then when do you want to come back?" Dallas asked.

Grant shook his head. "I can come back whenever you think I should."

"Well, I'd give it at least a week to ten days to heal."

"Then let's meet for dinner while it's healing," Grant stated.

Oh lord. He was starting already. We had been in the shop less than 15 minutes, and he was already flirting. *"So much for this,"* I mumbled.

"For what? What were you expecting?" Ivan asked from the floor.

I lifted my head off my paws and gazed down at him. *"He's flirting. And he's very bad at flirting. And she smells nice, and he needs a woman in his life, but he's just going to screw it up again."*

I watched Ivan's ear twitch. *"And she has a bad track record of picking men who are...how you say it? Глупый."*

"Huh?" Okay, so there was a bit of a language barrier between Ivan and me. His thick accent didn't help.

"Stupid."

"Why didn't you just say that?" I asked. I wiggled my way towards the end of the tattoo chair and looked down at Ivan. I put my head on my paws.

"I am still learning your language."

"Oh." I swear, I'm surrounded by idiots.

We both looked up as Grant laughed about something and Dallas smiled, leaning in to start working on his tattoo. I saw the swift look that passed between them. It was a shy look of attraction on Dallas' face, a goofy grin that typically led to that six-pack of Pabst I mentioned earlier on Grant's.

"Hey, pampered pooch. My servant is undressing your master with her eyes. Can he care for her?"

I turned away from the scene, noticing how every so often Dallas would gaze up at Grant with a soft look on her face. *"He sure can."*

"Da, then we must make sure this happens."

I jumped down from the chair and went to sit next to Ivan. We watched Grant and Dallas talk, seeing the adoring looks they gave each other. We could smell their pheromones. *"How?"*

"By staging an intervention."

I looked at Ivan. *"I'm listening."*

Memoirs of a Pomsky

Conversations At the Clubhouse

If I had known what an intervention was, I would definitely not have agreed to staging one with Ivan's help. First off, he's a cat. Now, I don't know about the rest of you, but cats are not my cup of tea, coffee, juice or water. But he is bigger than me and I'm really scared that he's going to sit on me and crush me.

That's beside the point. According to what Ivan was telling me, Dallas hasn't been on a date in a good...over a thousand days. I don't remember the exact number he told me. I've slept since then. But that's, like, forever! How can someone as sweet and kind and gentle as her not have a date? I would blame the cat, but even he is worried.

And cats don't worry.

So far, Grant has had four sessions with Dallas and gone on a few dates with her. We picked her up one night on the Harley and went cruising around town. He took her to his favorite drive through – I got a pup cup of cream...yummy! And for the most part, the date seemed to go well. Ivan wasn't too thrilled that I got to go, and he didn't, but can you see him in a pair of motorcycle goggles?

"Please. They would ruffle my fur."

See?

I had hoped we were going on another date with Dallas tonight, but it's meeting night for the Drunken Outlaws Motorcycle Club. Since Dallas wasn't exactly dating my master, it was just the two of us. Grant set me down in the grass outside the clubhouse so I could "do my business" and I waited until he walked over to a few of the guys before sniffing around.

Doggo was here. So was Perry. Mason. Linus and Lucy...they are Chihuahua siblings. And someone I hadn't met yet.

"Hey, Delphine. Come over and meet the new guy!"

That's Doggo. He's a pit bull from the Bronx with one eye and a mangy coat. He's a sweet guy. Just very rough around the edges. He's had a hard life, but his master spoils him and he deserves it. *"Hey Doggo. What's shaking?"*

"This is Clint. He's Tony's new pal."

I looked at Clint and gave his butt the quick sniff in greeting and he returned the favor. *"Nice to meet you."*

"Hey, I hear Laslow has a new dame," Perry commented. *"Is it true? Has he given her a six-pack of Pabst yet?"*

I couldn't help but sigh as I sat down next to Doggo. *"No, he hasn't. He took her to the drive through but that's been about it. Went to the wharf and watched the boats go by as they talked. Invited her to the office for lunch, but no Pabst yet."*

"Where'd he find this dame anyway?"

Who the hell used the word "dame" in this day and age? *"She's a tattoo artist. She's the one giving dad his new ink. They liked each other from the day he walked in the shop. I could tell. The room got very whiffy."*

The others all went "Oh" like a bunch of puppies.

"Is she nice? Did she give you treats?" Lucy asked.

"I like her. She has soft hands, and she loves to bury her face in my fur. She lets me give her kisses and giggles when I do." I paused. I debated on whether or not I should admit my only problem with Dallas. I decided to go for it. I laid down in the cool grass and put my head on my paws. *"The only thing is...she has a cat."*

"What's a cat?" Linus asked.

A low growl came from the shadows behind Doggo. The only member of our little canine circle that kept to himself and never said much. Zeus. He's a brindle boxer who, for the most part, is a big love. But you threaten any of us or his master, all bets are off. *"Cat. Felis catus. A small, domesticated carnivorous mammal that thinks it's better than everyone and everything around them. They think they are gods. Humans are nothing to them but servants that come and go at their whim."* He slowly walked into the light. *"Their claws are sharp, as is their tongues."* He slowly bared his teeth. *"And they are very tasty for dinner."*

Okay. To be fair Zeus makes cats sound like they are some sort of demon spawn. Maybe they are. Maybe not. *"Can we get back on the subject? My master's new lady friend?"*

"What about her, little Delphine?" Zeus rumbled.

"How do I get them to stay together?" I paused, jumping up and turning in a circle. *"Laslow is horrible at dating. You guys know that."* I couldn't help a small whimper.

Zeus snorted and returned to his spot behind us. *"Start by getting rid of the cat."*

That's useful advice. Not.

Before I could tell them more about the predicament I was in with trying to make sure Grant hooked up with Dallas and kept her around, we were called into the clubhouse by our owners. I slowly trotted up the stairs, my mind going over everything. I really liked Dallas. I really needed Grant to hurry up and make his move.

Before I could finish my thoughts, he scooped me up and carried me into the clubhouse with a kiss to the top of my head. I looked up and licked his chin. I do so love my master.

I just want him to be happy.

Memoirs of a Pomsky

It Was Going So Well

I sat on the little bed Dallas bought for me and was happily dozing while Grant was getting work done on his tattoo. This was the fifth session and so far, things were going well. Turns out, Dallas happens to like Pabst Blue Ribbon (why? Blech!), Slim Jim's and pork rinds. She was also a big fan of the stock car races and I spent the entire weekend on her lap as they watched the Brickyard 400 on Grant's big screen television.

I still can't figure out what the obsession was with making left hand circles.

It was also the first weekend Dallas stayed the night. I knew what was coming when she gently placed me on the floor and leaned in to kiss Grant. She made the first move! It was a quick kiss on the lips before she stood and walked to the kitchen, but a kiss is a kiss is a kiss! I followed her, my tail going a mile a minute as she rummaged in the fridge for some more salsa. She leaned down to pet me, and I couldn't help but plop over and show her my belly.

"Somebody wants belly scratches," Dallas crooned.

What? I'm not beyond being a little...pushy when I want a belly rub. Don't judge.

When the race was over, Grant offered to take Dallas home, but she told him she had a better idea, took his hand and led him to the bedroom. I thought for sure she was going to close the door on me, but instead, she scooped me up and carried me inside.

I was right about Dallas doing yoga, too. She got up very early the next morning and went to the deck off of Grant's room to do it. She even let me stay there with her. "Yoga with a sweet puppy like you is going to be so much fun, Miss Delphine," she chuckled. Her smile is as bright as the sun, and I couldn't help giving her kisses while she was in downward dog.

Now, I was dozing in my own bed at Pigments of Your Imagination, Ivan snoring in his bed next to me. Ivan and I have a small truce between us, especially after I filled him in on the details of what happened that night. Let's just say I pulled my own blanket over my head that night. The moon was full, if you catch my drift, and my little innocent eyes didn't need to see it.

The door to the shop opened and I lifted my head, letting out a little bark at the bell. I stood up, stretched and turned around, laying back down. That was when I caught the smell. It was a nauseating combination of alcohol and weed mixed with body odor and general malaise. I looked at Ivan. His ears were back, and he was growling. *"Who is that?"* I asked the cat.

"No one good," he growled back. *"Dallas'
ex-boyfriend, Matt."*

I didn't like this guy, and I hadn't even
laid eyes on him yet. I let out a soft bark and
growl as I watched Dallas walk around the short
wall that separated the main part of the parlor
and her workstation. I followed her, Ivan
jumping up onto the wall and perching
menacingly on the corner. I sat below him and
barked at the new guy.

"What are you doing here, Matt?" Dallas
asked. She was not happy that the man was in
her shop.

Matt ran his fingers through his hair and
smiled sheepishly at Dallas. "Hey Dal. I...uh...I
just thought I'd swing by and see how you were."

"I'm great. What are you doing here?"

I watched as this guy walked up to Dallas
and tried to give her a kiss. She pushed him
away and I gave a low growl. His ragged jeans
smelled as dank as he did, and I really did not
like the vibes this guy was giving off.

"I wanted to let you know I was out."

Dallas folded her arms across her chest. It was a stance that made humans closed off and I could tell she really didn't want this guy here. "Okay. So, you're out. What of it?" she snapped.

"Well, I was hoping we could pick up where we left off and maybe...you know...give me my job back."

"Not on your life," Ivan growled.

Dallas reached out and scratched his head in a soothing manner. "It's okay Ivan. I know you don't like him." She leaned over to kiss the top of his furry head. "Matt, I told you the day I came to the jail to meet you that we were done and not to come back here."

I heard Grant shift behind me, his heavy footfall on the tiled floor. Oh boy. If Grant was getting involved, it was not going to work out well for this Matt fella. I looked up at my master, leaning into his jean clad leg. I let out a little bark, my fur standing up. I barked again, bouncing once or twice.

"Hey, pooch. You look stupid. Not intimidating," Ivan said from his perch above me.

I didn't care. I meant business.

"Aw, c'mon Dallas. I need the work. My probation officer said I need to be employed and all I know how to do is this. Besides, half of this shop belongs to me," Matt pressured.

"No, it doesn't. I sent you the legal documents stating that I was buying out your share. Your lawyer has it."

"Then where is the money?" Matt snapped.

"Why don't you ask your lawyer?" She motioned toward the door with a dismissive wave of her hand. "So, it's time for you to leave."

"You can't do this to me," he begged.

"Hey buddy. The lady asked you to leave."

Matt looked at Grant and stepped towards Dallas. It was on then. Ivan swiped at the man, hissing loudly and leaving a line of red welts down his bare arm. Matt stepped back, unsure what to think. Ivan growled and stood, looking like at Halloween cat as he hissed. "Fucking cat!" Matt snapped. "Damn thing probably gave me rabies or something. You need to lock it up. That thing is wild."

"That is what you get for trying to touch my servant," Ivan hissed.

"Okay, buddy. It's time for you to go. The lady asked you nicely and now I'm telling you to leave. You're cutting into my time." Grant stepped forward and took a hold of Matt by the arm. "Let's go before Miss Dallas calls the cops."

I was surprised to see Matt go with my master without a fight. I danced around Dallas' feet in the hopes she would pick me up. She did, burying her face in my fur as she pet Ivan with her other hand.

"My two protectors," she sighed. "Thank you both." She set me down on my bed and opened the drawer she kept the treats in, retrieving some for each of us.

I settled in to eat the Greenie bone she had given me when I heard my master's voice raise. He was still outside with that Matt guy. Ivan and I glanced at each other. *"That doesn't sound good."*

"He just threatened my servant."

"I know. My dad didn't like that."

"Neither did she."

We both watched as Dallas marched to the door, her cell phone in hand. She was calling the police. It didn't take long for them to show up and she chased Grant back into the shop. He scooped me up and sat in the chair, petting me roughly. He was itching for a fight, I could tell, and it was going to take him some time to calm back down.

I wasn't sure I would have any fur left by the time he did.

When Dallas came back in, she was very quiet. She looked like she had been crying as she sat back down next to Grant. She picked up the tattoo gun, carefully putting me back on the floor. I went back to eating my bone, but the tension between them was thick. Did Grant do something to upset Dallas? He was just being chivalrous, making that Matt guy leave.

"I think we need to make the next appointment for next month. My schedule is getting full," Dallas finally said.

Grant gazed at her. "Okay. We still on for dinner next week? Our usual date?"

Dallas bit her lower lip and leaned in as she worked. "I'll let you know. I looked at my online scheduler and it's getting crazy."

Ivan stopped chewing his claws, lowering his leg as he gazed over at me. *"Remember that intervention I mentioned when we first met?"*

I remembered. *"Yeah, why?"*

"Because we may need it very soon."

Beth A. Freely

You're Not Ross and Rachel

Next month, which was only two weeks from the day Matt showed up at Pigments of Your Imagination, turned into six weeks. And then ten. And then twelve. No matter what my master did, Miss Dallas wasn't biting. She didn't want to come over and watch the races. She didn't want to go for a ride on the Harley and she didn't want to chat when he came in to have work done on his tattoo. It was like their romance came to a screeching halt when Matt came into the shop and Grant said something to him.

I guess Grant thought that they were more of an item than they were? I honestly don't know what happened. I do know that Grant was very bummed out and...well...sulking. That's the only word I can think of. And again, he was turning me into a margarita glass with the amount of crying he was doing into my fur.

I sat in my little bed in Grant's office contemplating the bowl of kibble in front of me when I heard his cellphone ring. I was about to get up when I saw him sit up in his office chair.

"Hey, hey, what's wrong? Dallas, sweetheart, please, take a deep breath. Okay. Take another one. That's it. Now, what's the matter?"

I couldn't stop my tail from wagging knowing she had called my master. This was a good sign. Maybe they weren't like Ross and Rachel. Maybe they really weren't on a break.

Okay, I watched "Friends." Sue me. I happen to like that show.

"Yes. Yes, I will take care of him. I'm sure Delphine won't mind. She'll probably be a bit miffed at first, but they'll get along. You take care of what you need to. I'll take care of Ivan."

He paused. "It's okay. We'll talk when you get back. Yes, I've missed you too, but I agree, in hindsight, I crossed the line." He paused again. "Do you need money for the flight? Let me fly you out there. You're in no shape to drive. Okay. I've got meetings the rest of the afternoon. Come by the office and ask for my secretary, Abby. She'll take Ivan and let him in my office."

Ivan was coming here? I was going to have to share my doggie bed with him? My private space was about to smell like cat!

"You missed me."

"No, Ivan, I didn't."

Well, maybe a little. But don't tell him that.

Grant popped out of his office after hanging up with Dallas and I heard him talking to Abby. Apparently, we had a corporate jet that I didn't know about. Not that my master went anywhere without me most of the time. He was telling Abby where Dallas needed to go and was providing the jet for her.

See? He really, really likes her!

I took a few bites of kibble, my eavesdropping done, when he came back into the office. He knelt down by me and ruffled my fur as I ate.

"We're gonna have a houseguest for a week or two," Grant said. "Miss Dallas' dad passed away suddenly, and she needs to fly home to make all the arrangements." I sat back on my haunches and looked at him.

"You probably have no idea what I'm saying, do you princess?"

"Yes, I do," I barked.

Grant laughed. "Okay, pumpkin, maybe you do. Ivan is going to come stay with us. Can you be nice to him?"

"Do I have to be nice?" I asked.

Grant laughed again and gave my butt a little scratch. "That's my girl. I knew you could be nice. I know he's a cat, but you two seem to get along well."

That wasn't exactly what I was hinting at, but okay. I'd have to put up with the Russian

Blue for a few weeks. He was going to have to live by my rules. It was my house, not his.

And one thing was for sure. He wasn't sleeping on Grant's bed.

If I had to put up with Ivan, then I better get belly rubs. I rolled over and waited. Grant didn't disappoint.

The Housepest

"What does "passed away" mean?" I asked my friends at the clubhouse. It was a "No Cats Allowed" kind of club, so Ivan was stuck at home. He'd been there for a week, and I could not handle him moping about the way he did. He was as bad as Grant. I get that he was missing Dallas but talk about a drama queen!

Zeus lifted his leg and relieved himself on his favorite tree before walking over to us. He sat down, chewed his leg for a moment and then huffed. *"It means that someone or something has crossed the Rainbow Bridge. They are chasing rabbits in the sky."*

"Or foxes," Doggo added. *"Why you asking Delph?"*

I walked over to sit next to Zeus. He made me feel safe. "Cause Laslow and I are babysitting that stupid cat cause Dallas' dad passed away."

"Ah," Zeus growled. *"So, it was a human that passed away. A sad day for any companion they may have had."* The other dogs all nodded in agreement. Zeus sniffed the top of my head and gave me a little lick. *"It is kind of Laslow to watch the kitty."*

"He does nothing but sulk, Zeus. He lays around sleeping all day and then walks around meowing this pitiful...noise. I can't stand it. He's driving me crazy. I'm losing my fur because of it."

I am, too. Grant says I'm shedding my winter coat, but I think it's because I'm stressed. Ivan is making me anxious. I can't handle it! Plus, there is no amount of catnip in this world to mellow him out. And he's sleeping on the bed!

Zeus chuckled. *"He is missing his servant, Delphine. Cats have separation anxiety. They do not like to be away from their humans for long. They are not like us. They do not travel well and require much maintenance."*

"Yeah, like litter boxes. Did he bring a litter box? Have you tried the litter treats yet?" Perry asked. He spun around in a circle. *"Litter treats are the bomb!"*

Doggo stared at Perry. *"You do realize that litter treats are just cat shit, right?"*

"Yeah!"

Perry was way too happy about the idea of eating litter treats. I shook my head, amazed that he kissed his owner with that mouth.

"Boys, there is a lady present." Zeus laid down and nudged me with his nose. *"Delphine, I know you are kindly tolerating this cat that has invaded your home. But he is missing his servant. Be nice to him. Right now, he needs a friend. And that friend could become your mistress. I heard Laslow talking with my master about Dallas. He is very taken by her, and he will do anything for her. If you help him*

care for this feline, then you will be looked upon kindly by her."

I thought about Zeus' words. He was right. If I was nice to Ivan, then maybe Miss Dallas would stay. To be honest, I missed her too. I missed going on long rides with her and Grant. I missed how she buried her face in my fur and how she let me do yoga with her on the back porch. I looked up at Zeus. He was right. *"Okay. I'll be nice to him."*

Zeus licked my head. *"That's a good Delphine. Who knows? Maybe we can make him an honorary dog if Laslow and Dallas stay together."*

"He's big enough," I mumbled. Someone whistled from the clubhouse, ending the conversation. When I get home, I will sit down and talk with Ivan.

And hopefully cheer him up.

We Interrupt This Memoir...

Ivan here. I'm hijacking this memoir because I need to get something off my chest. Hold on a second.

Sounds of a cat hacking up a hairball

That's better. I have a confession to make. Delphine says I talk with a thick accent, a Russian accent to be exact. Well...

I'm not Russian. Yeah, I'm a Russian Blue cat, but I'm not really from Russia. I'm from Paramus, New Jersey. I was the runt of the litter. I was adopted by an old Russian couple, and that was how I learned how to speak the language. But they couldn't take care of me as they got older, so Dallas adopted me.

And now...now...she's left me here with this...this...dog! I just want to die!

Look, Grant is cool and all, but I need my Dallas. She knows how to scratch my head the way I like. I need my nails trimmed. I've run out of my favorite kibble and this junk Grant is feeding me sucks!!!

I am laying here pathetically on my back on the bed. I am in kitty depression. I cannot handle being alone. Dallas takes me everywhere. I have a nice nest in her SUV. A soft blanket. Catnip.

Dramatic kitty sigh

I'm going to diiiiieeeee if Dallas doesn't come home...

Wait...do I smell...is that...

CATNIP!

"Ivan! Ivan, we stopped at the store! We got you stuff!"

Delphine came running into the bedroom and I plopped back down, giving her my most pathetic cat looks ever. *"Delphine. I am dying. I cannot go on."* I let my tongue loll out of my mouth.

"Get up, Ivan! Come on. You're not dying. I know you miss Dallas, but you're not dying. She'll be back soon." Delphine jumped up and down, trying to see me. I moved to the edge of the bed and gazed down at her. *"C'mon. Come see what we got you!"*

I sighed and jumped off the bed. I really did want the catnip. I lazily followed her into the living room and stopped. Before me, in front of the big bay window, was the most amazing cat tree. Grant was putting the final touches on it, and I sat there and watched. The kibble was my favorite, there were mouse toys and catnip balls and I thought I would cry.

"Oh my god, are you purring?" Delphine asked.

"Yeah, yeah I'm purring." I walked over to Grant and began to weave in and out of his legs before jumping up onto the cat tree. I

climbed to the top and loafed up in the box, surveying the world around me.

"*What happened to your accent?*" Delphine asked me. She caught on.

"*I'm actually from Jersey. The Russian accent makes me sound tough.*"

Delphine snorted. "*Poser.*"

"*Whatever.*" I kept purring before curling up into a ball and going to sleep.

There Is Hope

I'm taking my memoir back from Ivan. This silly cat had the nerve to hijack my memoir! He's such a jerk.

But I'm glad he did because now I know what is bothering him. Zeus was right. He is missing Dallas. My master is currently giving him a good brushing on the bed while I finish my bath on my pillow. We played the afternoon away since Grant didn't have to go into the office. I know it helped and he isn't pouting quite as much. I know the catnip helped him. It definitely mellowed him out.

I curled up into a ball and watched his eyes just get heavier. Grant's phone rang and he reached out, answering it. He put it on speakerphone. "Hey Dallas. How are things going?"

"Better than I hoped. Dad had left instructions so that made it easier to deal with on that front, but it's still hard," she replied. Dallas' voice sounded tired. I stood up and walked over to Ivan, lying down next to him. I began to lick his ears as we listened to the conversation between Grant and Dallas.

"How are you holding up?" Grant asked, stretching out on the bed.

"I'm okay. I'm sad. I miss dad and this was unexpected." She paused. "How's Ivan? Is he doing okay at your house?"

"Yeah. He's doing okay. He seems a bit bummed out and missing you, but Delphine and I went to the pet store the other day and I got him some stuff." He grinned, picking up a cat toy with a long string and feather at the end. "He seems to be doing better," Grant added as he bounced the toy up and down. Ivan couldn't resist batting at it, and I moved back to my pillow.

"You're not spoiling him, are you?"

Grant kept bouncing the toy. "Never."

Pft. He was spoiling Ivan. However, with that being said, I was getting spoiled too. I got a plethora of new bones and chew toys. Ivan actually played fetch, so I was willing to share them with him. He was a very odd cat, to be sure.

"Grant, listen. I'm sorry about how I acted after the incident with Matt. I know you were just trying to be protective." She fell silent for a moment. "I've...I've never had anyone do that before and I didn't know how to take it."

My master reached out and began to scratch my head. "Hey, I get it, Dallas. I might've come on a bit too strong as well." I licked his fingers as he kept talking. "I'm not used to having a girl be into racing and like Pabst or riding on my bike. You're really cool and, to be honest, I miss watching you do yoga on my deck in the mornings."

I missed doing it with her. I wonder if he noticed that...

"I think Delphine misses doing yoga with you too," Grant added.

Yup. He noticed.

Dallas was silent for a few moments. "Grant, when I get back, let's go back to the way it was before Matt showed up. I like our rides. I like feeling the wind on my face and wrapping my arms around you. I love little Delphine and I know you love Ivan, even though he can be a royal pain."

Ivan opened an eye. *"I am not a pain,"* he meowed in protest. He stood up, stretched and jumped off the bed. *"I'm going to go leave litter treats."*

Thanks for the warning. I watched my master, waiting to see what he had to say about her words. I couldn't resist wagging my tail. I looked up at him expectantly. Say yes, Grant. C'mon, say yes. Say yes.

Grant sat up. "Yeah, Dal, yeah. I want to go back to the way it was. I miss you. I've done my fair share of sulking with Ivan over the last few weeks. And everyone in the club is dying to meet you. They think you'd be a great addition to the group. And I love the way you cling to me when we ride. And how you laugh when I tell you a bad joke."

Yes! I started doing happy circles on the bed. They were going to get back together! I could go back to the tattoo shop and get treats, lay in my comfy bed and torment Ivan. I yipped happily, and I could hear Dallas laughing on the other end of the phone. *"Ivan! Ivan! Get in here!"*

Ivan wondered in languidly and jumped back up on the bed. *"What did I miss?"*

"Your mom and my master are getting back together! When she gets back! They are going to talk and start dating again."

Ivan gave me a long slow blink. *"Yay,"* he replied without any enthusiasm. Yet I could tell that he was happy about it. His big eyes twinkled as he lifted his leg to bathe. I could hear his purr from here.

I settled back down on my pillow and listened to the rest of the conversation between Grant and Dallas. I loved hearing the way they laughed at each other's jokes, and they talked about mundane things that didn't mean anything to Ivan or me. He was still grooming, and I decided to do something I've never done before. I shifted on my pillow and looked at the cat.

"Hey Ivan."

"What?"

"You...you want to share my pillow?" I asked.

Ivan lifted his head and stared at me. "You want...me to share your pillow?"

"Sure. C'mon."

Ivan paused and stared at me. Grant and Dallas ended their phone call and I watched as he turned off the light to the nightstand, plunging the bedroom into darkness. After a few moments, I felt Ivan step onto my pillow. I wasn't worried about him laying on me anymore. Instead, he curled up into a tight ball.

After a while, his head was upside down and he was purring. I put my head on my paws, Ivan's fur tickling my whiskers. It wasn't long before I, too, fell asleep.

52

Operation Kiss the Girl

"Are you ready?" I asked Ivan. *"She'll be here any moment."*

"Yes. Yes. You just worry about doing all the jumping and barking. I'll do all the weaving. We will make sure they kiss and kiss deeply." Ivan sat there cleaning his face with one delicate paw. He put his paw down and gazed at me through slitted eyes. *"Grant didn't actually buy me a pair of goggles, did he?"*

I giggled. *"I'll never tell."*

Grant did buy Ivan a pair of goggles. And a little backpack bubble so he could ride with us.

He really wanted to include the cat in family activities, regardless of Ivan's thoughts on the matter. It would be interesting to see what it was going to take to put those goggles on the cat.

I heard a car door and I started to wag my tail. Grant threw open the door and Dallas stepped inside. As soon as she did, Ivan started meowing and weaving in and out of her legs. I started jumping up and down, like one of those bouncy spring dogs you see in toy shops. I couldn't help but bark as well.

"Welcome back, Dallas. We've got so much to tell you. Ivan has a new cat tree and new toys, and we play fetch together and he's very good at catching balls. Better than me," I told her.

Dallas wasn't sure who she should pay attention to first, Ivan or me. She took a step forward and Ivan struck. The world slowed down as we stepped back and watched.

Dallas tripped over Ivan.

She was falling towards Grant.

Grant reached out, his arms slipping around her waist.

He caught her before she could fall to the floor.

There was a look that passed between them...

A soft look of affection...

I held my breath. Ivan leaned forward in anticipation. I was shaking in hope.

And then it happened.

They kissed.

Not just a quick kiss like we'd seen before. This was a real kiss. Grant cupped the back of Dallas' head, his other arm wrapping around her waist. She slipped her arms around his neck and leaned into the kiss. She lifted one foot up, like some old romantic movie. Grant broke the kiss for a moment, gazed at her and leaned in to kiss her again.

THIS is what Ivan and I had been waiting for. This was the kiss we needed to see.

"So...I guess we are stuck with each other, da?" Ivan asked, slipping back into his Russian accent.

I thought about it for a moment as I watched my master...my dad...kissing Dallas.

Grant ended the kiss. "You know, I can honestly say that I love you."

Dallas smiled up at him. She cupped his cheek and leaned back in to him. "I love you too." She kissed him softly, sliding her hand in his.

Ivan and I stood there and watched as Dallas tugged Grant towards the bedroom. "Do you think your place is big enough for Ivan and Delphine and us?" she asked.

Grant looked back at us. "Yeah. Yeah, it's big enough." He stepped backwards into the bedroom, Dallas following him. Grant looked at Ivan and me. "You two kids behave, okay?" He winked at me, and I wagged my tail as I watched him close the door.

"I'm going to go take a nap in the sun," Ivan stated as he walked towards his cat tree. *"You can nap in my bed."*

I really hated it when I couldn't go into the bedroom. After all, that satin pillow at the head of the bed was mine. But you know what? It was okay. I was willing to share my pillow with Dallas and Ivan.

Even though he was a cat.

I followed him into the living room and gazed up at him in the top bed of the cat tree. Ivan was already asleep and purring. I settled into his bed.

All was right in my world. My master finally found love.

And I found a best friend.

"Even though I am a cat?"

"Even though you're a cat."

THE END...MAYBE

About The Author

Award-winning author Beth A. Freely was born and raised in upstate New York, with a brief and very influential stint living in Great Britain that can be seen in her writing. Today she calls New Mexico home. When asked how long she has been writing, she'll tell you, "All my life."

In 2003, she published some of her fanfiction online and won awards for her stories. Two years later, she was the 1st Place winner of the 2005 Arche Books Publishing Novel Writing Contest in Women's Fiction with her novel *Behind the Eyes of Dorian Gray*. In 2022, she took home 1st Place in Romance/Science-Fiction and 2nd Place in Science-Fiction/Aliens

Beth A. Freely

& Alien Invasion in the Spring Bookfest Awards with her novel *Beyond The Steps of Stone.*

Beth holds a masters in English and Creative Writing and enjoys horseback riding, swimming, reading, cuddling her cats, and helping other authors hone their craft.

Memoirs of a Pomsky

Read More of Beth's Books

Behind The Eyes Of Dorian Gray
The Legend Of Captain St Pierre
The Loch
Beyond The Steps Of Stone

Story Stories/Novellas
Brace For Impact
A Taste Of Nostalgia